GOOD ROSIE!

KATE DiCAMILLO

PICTURES BY
HARRY BLISS

WALKER BOOKS
AND SUBSIDIARIES
LONDON · BOSTON · SYDNEY · AUCKLAND

First published 2018 by Walker Books Ltd
87 Vauxhall Walk, London SE11 5HJ

2 4 6 8 10 9 7 5 3 1

Text © 2018 Kate DiCamillo

Illustrations © 2018 Harry Bliss

The right of Kate DiCamillo and Harry Bliss to be identified as the author and
illustrator respectively of this work has been asserted by them in
accordance with the Copyright, Designs and Patents Act 1988

This book has been typeset in Myriad Pro

Printed in China

British Library Cataloguing in Publication Data:
a catalogue record for this book is available from the British Library

ISBN 978-1-4063-8357-7

www.walker.co.uk

For Ramona
and for Remy, Hazel, Louie, Agatha, Poppy and Fred
and for Henry, of course
K. D.

For Sofi, my beautiful muse
H. B.

Rosie lives with George.
Rosie is a good dog.

Every morning, Rosie and George eat breakfast together. George has two poached eggs. Rosie eats dog food from a big silver bowl.

When the bowl is empty, Rosie can see another dog staring back at her.

"Hello!" says Rosie.

Ruff!

"Hello?" says Rosie.

Ruff?

The other dog never answers.
That makes Rosie feel lonely.

But after breakfast, George says,

Rosie! Let's go for a walk.

A walk is a good thing.
A walk is not lonely at all.

PART TWO · THE CLOUDS

Rosie and George walk together.

Sometimes, Rosie chases squirrels.
She runs very fast, as fast as she can.
But she never catches anything.

Rosie, get back here!

Rosie always returns to George.

Good, Rosie. Good dog.

George thinks that most clouds look like historical figures.
Rosie thinks that most clouds look like squirrels.

One day, George sees something different in the clouds.

Look, Rosie! That one looks like a dog!

The cloud *does* look like a dog!
Rosie wags her tail.
"Hello, hello!" she shouts.

Woof, woof!

The dog cloud does not answer her.
Rosie feels lonely in an
empty-silver-bowl sort of way.

Something new is the dog park.

Isn't this great?
Look at all these dogs.

Rosie does not like the dog park.
There are too many dogs.
She doesn't know any of them.

It makes Rosie feel lonely to look at
so many strange dogs.

And a little bit afraid.

WOOF!

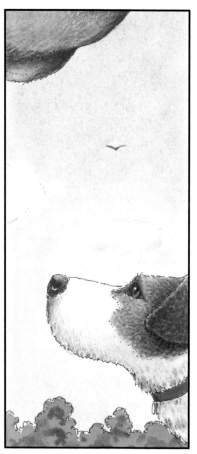

"My name is, uh, Maurice," says a very big dog. "And I have a bunny."

Rosie growls.

GRRRrrrr...

Rosie is not a bad dog.
She is a good dog.
But she can't help it.
She doesn't like Maurice.
Or his bunny.

Maurice shakes his stuffed bunny.
He shakes it very, very hard.

He drops the bunny on the ground.
Maurice says, "Wanna, uh, play bunny?"

"I want to go home,"
Rosie says to George.

But something is bouncing toward Rosie.
The something is a very small dog with a very sparkly collar.

YIP!
YIP!

"I'm Fifi! I'm Fifi!" says the small dog.
"It says *Fifi* right on my collar! See?
My name is spelled out in shiny stones.
What's your name?"

Rosie doesn't like the big, loud Maurice.
She doesn't like the small, yippy Fifi.
Rosie wants to go home.

YIP!

"Uh," Maurice says to Fifi, "do *you* want to play?"

"Me?" says Fifi.

Maurice wags his tail.

Maurice crouches.

Maurice pounces.

Somebody is Rosie.

"Ouch," says Maurice. He opens his mouth.
Fifi falls to the ground with a small thud.

Fifi says, "Am I alive?"
Rosie says, "Yes."

Fifi stands up. She wags her tail.

Her collar sparkles.
Her legs tremble.
She holds her tiny head up high
and says, "I'm Fifi and I'm alive!"

For the first time, Rosie likes Fifi.
Just a little bit.

Maurice coughs. He says, "Uh, gee."

He spits three tiny stones
onto the ground.

"Hey! Those are my shiny stones," says Fifi.

YIP!
YIP!
YIP!

You're not Fifi any more. You're Fif.

"I'm Fif?" says Fif.

"Sorry," says Maurice.

Fif says, "You tried to eat me! And now my name is Fif!"

"I just, uh, wanted to be friends," says Maurice.

YIP, YIP, YIPPI! YIP-YIP! YIP!

Rosie says, "That's not how you make friends!"

"Oh," says Maurice. "How do you, uh, do it, then?"

Rosie closes her eyes.
She thinks about her empty bowl.
She opens her eyes and looks up at the clouds in the sky.
"I don't know," says Rosie. "I'm not sure how you do it."

"Do you want to be friends with a dog named Fif?" Fif says to Rosie.

"I do," says Rosie. She is surprised to hear herself say it. "I do want to be friends with a dog named Fif."

"*That's* how you make friends," says Fif to Maurice.

Maurice says, "Uh, OK, would you be friends with a dog named Maurice? If he – uh, let's see – if he promised not to swallow any more of your tiny shiny things?"

Fif looks at Rosie. Rosie looks at Maurice.
"OK," says Rosie. "OK OK!" says Fif.

Had enough, Rosie?
Want to go home?

Rosie looks up at George.
She wags her tail …

and then
she sits down.

Rosie wants to stay.

In the morning, George eats two poached eggs. Rosie eats dog food out of her silver bowl.

When breakfast is over, George says,

Dog park, Rosie?

And Rosie walks away from her bowl without looking back.

At the dog park, Fif is waiting.
Maurice is waiting, too.

"Come on, Fif! Come on, Maurice!
Let's play!" says Rosie.

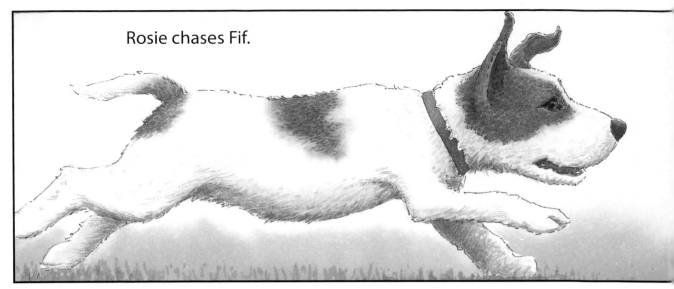

Rosie chases Fif.

They run very fast.

Maurice chases Rosie.

Sometimes, they catch each other.